FOX AND SQUIRREL
THE BEST
CHRISTMAS
EVER

Ruth Ohi

North Winds Press
An Imprint of Scholastic Canada Ltd.

Library and Archives Canada Cataloguing in Publication

Ohi, Ruth, author, illustrator
Fox and Squirrel, the best Christmas ever / Ruth Ohi.

ISBN 978-1-4431-5703-2 (hardback)

I. Title. II. Title: Best Christmas ever.

PS8579.H47F698 2016   jC813'.6   C2016-901028-7

www.scholastic.ca

Author photo: Debbie Ridpath-Ohi.

6 5 4 3 2 1   Printed in Malaysia 108   16 17 18 19 20

For Maeve and Charlie

"Snow!" said Fox. "This will be the best Christmas ever."

Squirrel agreed.

"There will be a party
with presents!"
said Squirrel.

"There will be red."

"And green."

"There will be fancy food!"

"Come and play,"
said Fox.

"No," said Squirrel. "I'm making the best Christmas ever."

"I can help," said Fox.

"NO!" said Squirrel. "Don't touch!
You'll ruin it."

11

"I won't ruin it,"
whispered Fox.

But Squirrel was off to find
more Christmas.

Deep in the forest,
Squirrel found more red.

Squirrel found more green.

But Squirrel could not find the way back.

"Uh-oh," said Squirrel.

"Look what I found!"
said Fox.

19

"I'm sorry I yelled!" yelled Squirrel.

"That's okay," said Fox. "Let's go home."

Walking along, they hummed a tune.

Fox hummed low.
Squirrel hummed high.

And once in a while, they
would meet in the middle.

"You tell the best stories,"
said Squirrel.

"And you are an excellent
dancer," said Fox.

"We're home," said Squirrel.
"Merry Christmas!"

"Merry Christmas,"
said Fox.

And it was.